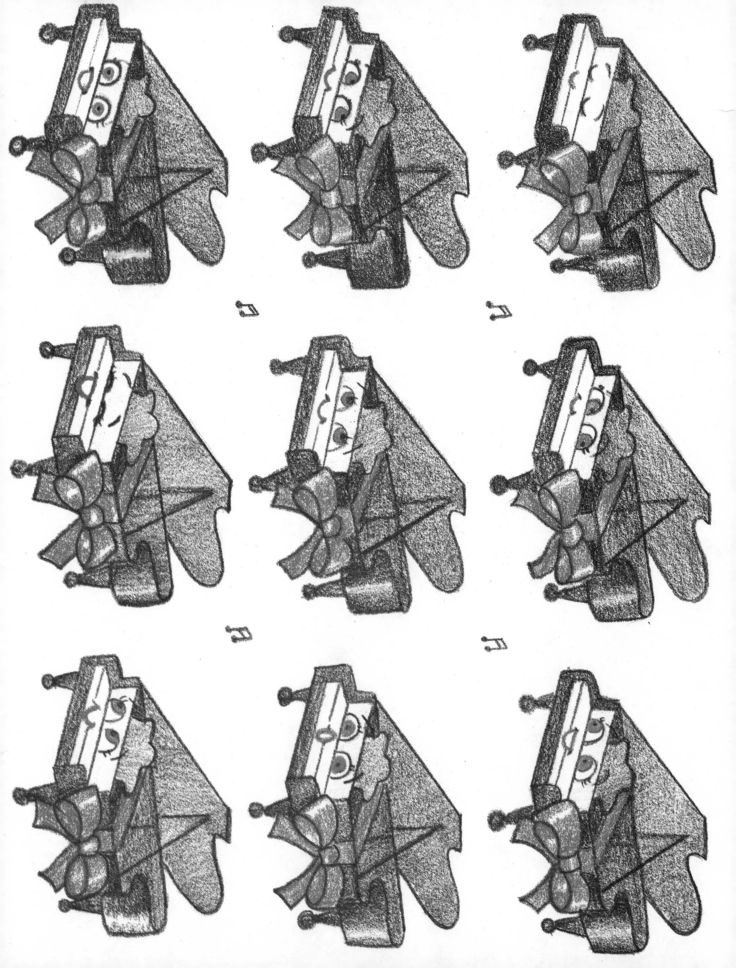

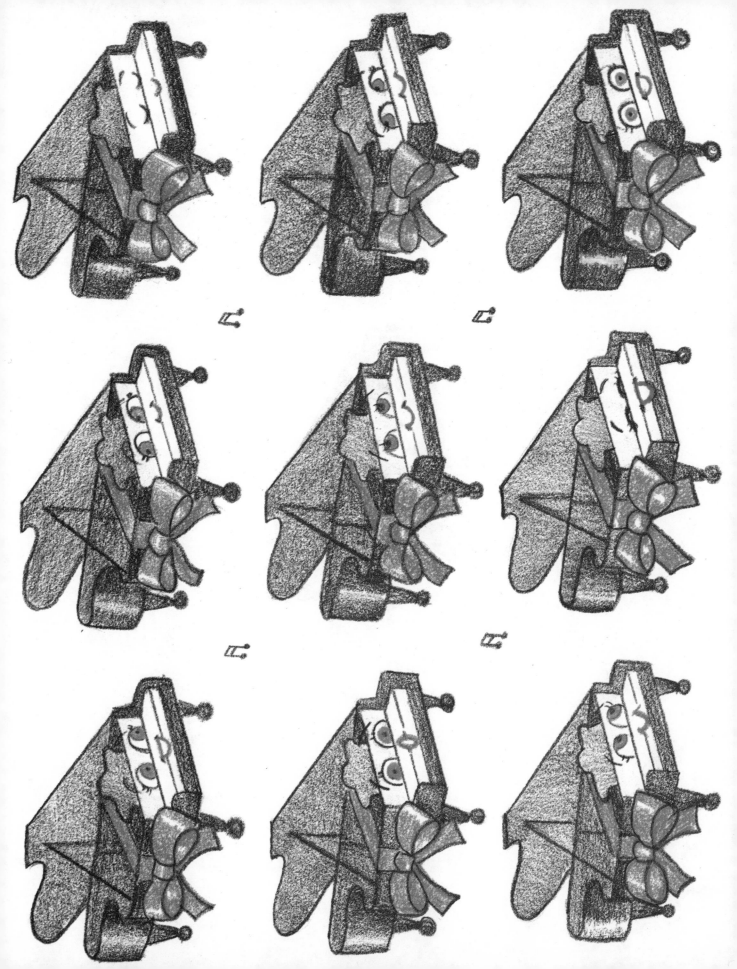

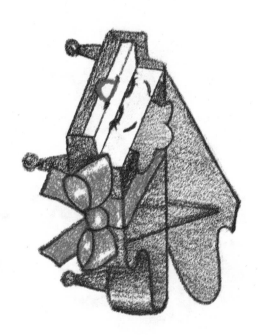

As she ran from the house toward her piano parade, Emma knew this was her HAPPIEST BIRTHDAY EVER!

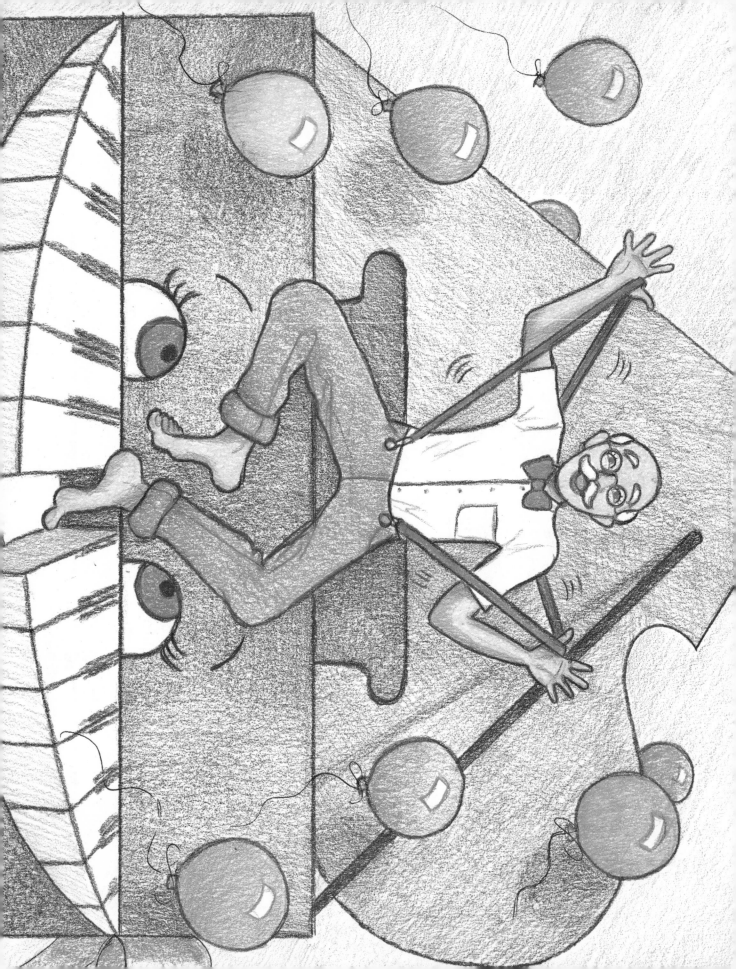

Emma Jane's dad was sitting atop the BIGGEST piano she had ever seen and playing it with his feet! And two rather tired delivery men were grunting and groaning in step with the music as they pushed the piano up the hill to Emma's house. Everyone was singing "HAPPY BIRTHDAY TO YOU!"

Then, she heard what sounded like a very loud parade. She ran to the window. Yes, a parade was coming up Peaksville Hill! Why, there was Edgar, using his cupcake pan as a drum. Betty Lou was playing her new flute.

There was no piano.
There must be some mistake she thought. After all, she had seen the big, red delivery truck parked in front of the house. And, this was her birthday. Well, she thought, it must be in another room! Yes, that's it! They are all hiding behind my new piano in another room. This must be a surprise party! But, she checked the rooms one by one and found no piano and no surprise party.

She reached her front door and closed her eyes very tightly. She opened her eyes when she entered the living room.

Meanwhile, Emma was making her way home from her school located at the very tippy top of Peaksville Hill. She practically flew down the hill toward home in excitement over the new piano.

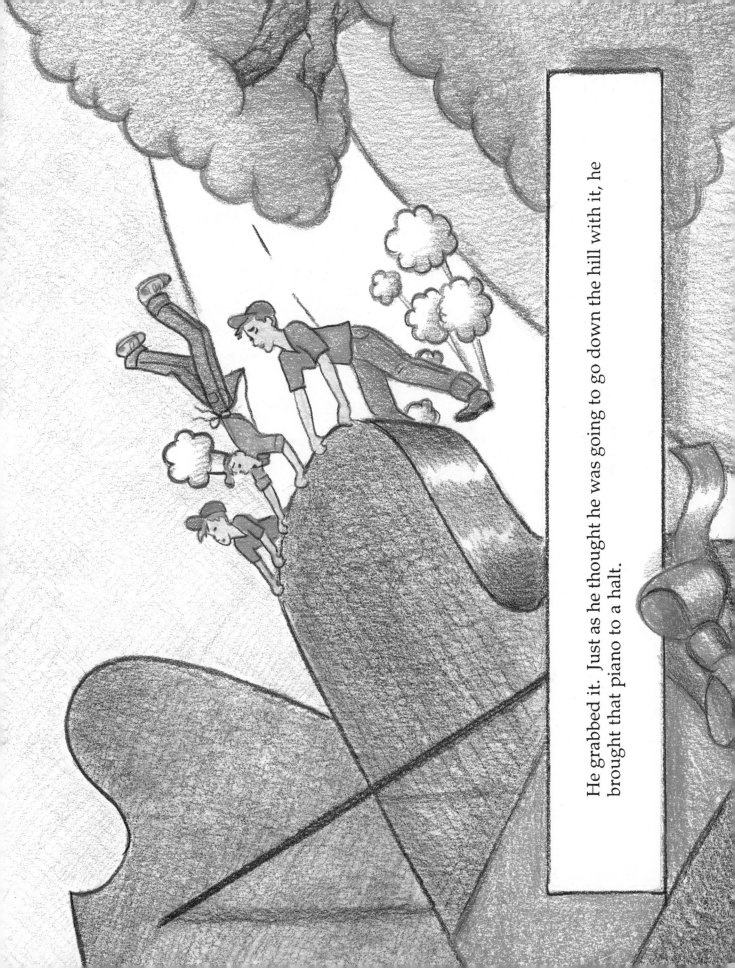

He grabbed it. Just as he thought he was going to go down the hill with it, he brought that piano to a halt.

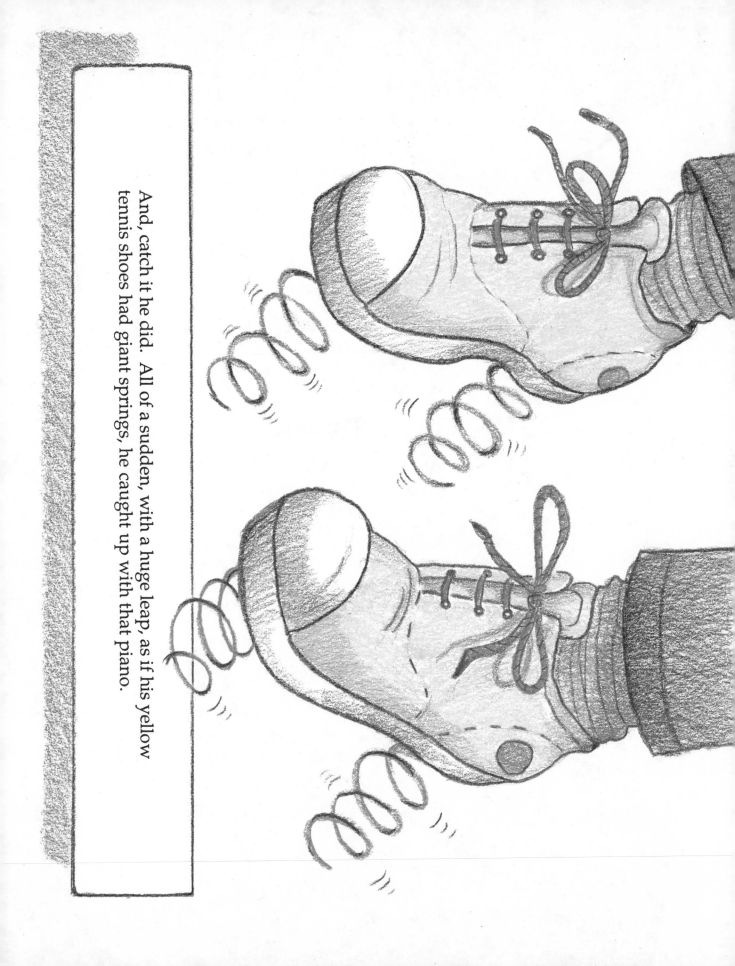

And, catch it he did. All of a sudden, with a huge leap, as if his yellow tennis shoes had giant springs, he caught up with that piano.

As Edgar ran, cupcakes began tumbling out of the pan. Soon, he was waving the empty pan high over his head, yelling, "Don't worry, Mr. Wipple! I'll catch your piano."

High School students on their way home from school joined the chase. Dogs barked and followed the group. A few squirrels even started scurrying along after the piano. The milkman joined in, with two folks who just left the dry cleaners. Betty Lou came straight from her music lesson, dropping everything she was carrying (except her flute) so she could run faster. (Her mother told her never to leave her NEW flute ANYWHERE.) Even the sheriff's son, Edgar, who was bringing a batch of birthday cupcakes up to Emma's house, started running.

THE GREAT PIANO CHASE!

The more they chased the piano, the faster it went.

"Come on everybody! We've got to stop it! We've just got to stop that piano!" yelled Mr Wipple.

The two rather small delivery men tried to stop the moving piano, but they ran smack into each other and fell flat on the sidewalk.

Suddenly, the piano started sliding:
right out of the truck, down the ramp,
down the street, and right down Peaksville Hill.

The truck screeched to a stop.
Two rather small men climbed out.
They yanked open the back doors of the truck,
and bounced the loading ramps down on the pavement.

All at once, they spotted a big, red truck winding its way up Peaksville Hill.

That day at school, Emma could hardly sit still. She couldn't wait to go home and see the piano.

The Wipples could hardly wait to see the piano, either. "Do you think it will really fit?" they kept asking each other as they waited for the delivery truck with Frank Cranks, their neighbor.

The day before Emma's birthday Mr. Wipple saw the ad for a piano. He could hardly believe his eyes! Arrangements were made to have the piano delivered the very next day.

The Wipples called friends. They called friends of friends. They checked the Peaksville Music Store. They even went to Fred's Friday Auction. There was not a piano to be found in Peaksville.

Mrs. Wipple would slowly shake her head 'no,' saying, "But Emma wants a piano so much. Everyday she comes home from school and runs to the living room looking for a piano. If we could somehow squeeze a piano into this house..."

"It would have to be a very small piano...." said Mr. Wipple.

"But, let's try it!" they both agreed at the very same time.

Mrs. Wipple certainly did talk to Mr. Wipple about the piano. She would talk about it over breakfast.

She would bring it up late at night when the household was very still.

But, the answer was always the same.

She would mention the piano when they chatted in the middle of the day.

"We just don't have room for a piano, Mildred. Do we? Do you think we have room?"

Emma told her tiny mother about the big piano. "Oh, Emma, such big ideas for such a little girl. Let me talk to your father about it," said Mrs. Wipple, whose small house was stacked with Wipples from top to bottom.

nce, around a birthday, Emma Jane Wipple, who was almost eight years old, decided she would like to have a piano. A big piano. She was sure that the bigger the piano, the louder and better the music would be.

for mom and dad

Emma's Happy Birthday Piano

by Bobbi McPeak Bailey

illustrated by Deborah DeFazio

The Wee Press
Terre Haute, Indiana

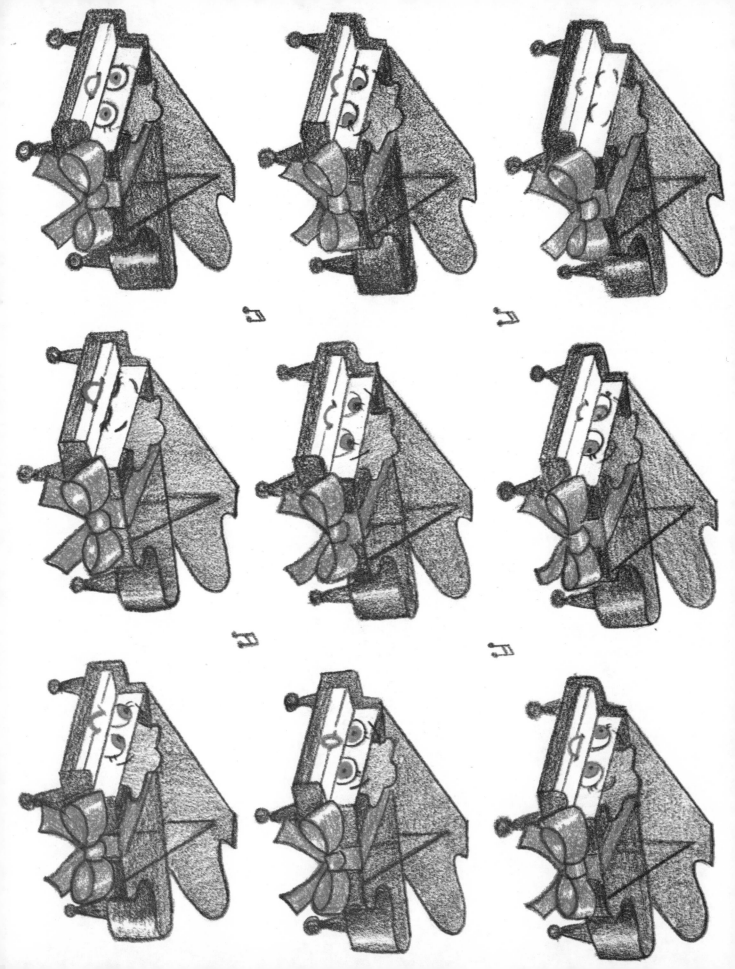

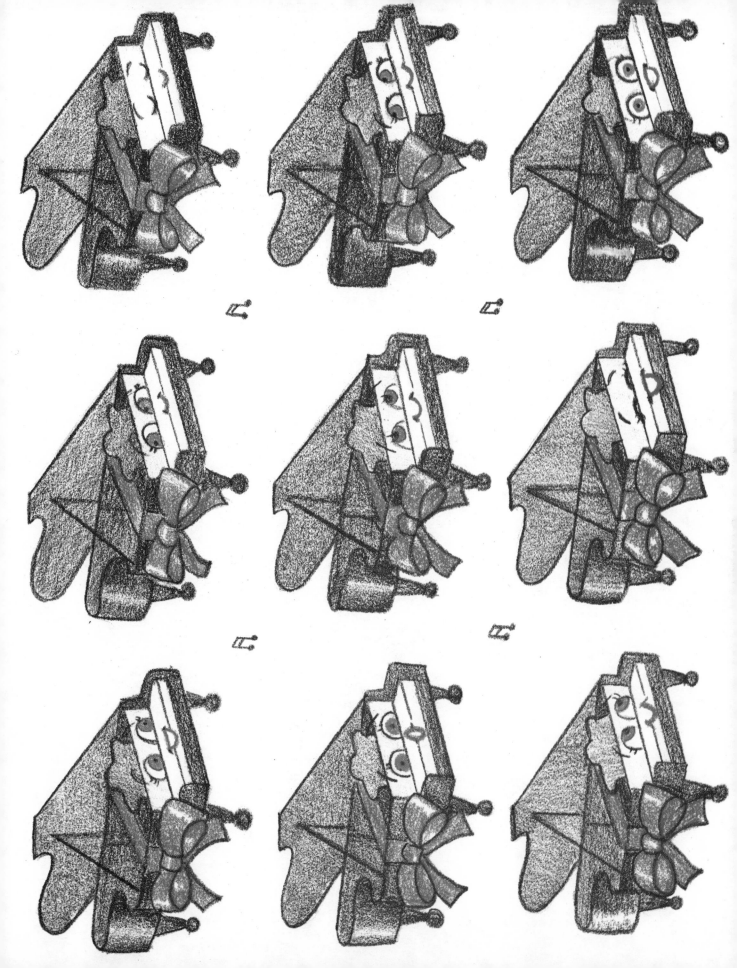

Yes for Piano.